This diary belongs to:

Pippa Morgan

KEEP OUT!

Scholastic Canada Ltd.
604 King Street West, Toronto, Ontario M5V 1E1, Canada

Scholastic Inc.
557 Broadway, New York, NY 10012, USA

Scholastic Australia Pty Limited
PO Box 579, Gosford, NSW 2250, Australia

Scholastic New Zealand Limited
Private Bag 94407, Botany, Manukau 2163, New Zealand

Scholastic Children's Books
Euston House, 24 Eversholt Street, London NW1 1DB, UK

www.scholastic.ca

Library and Archives Canada Cataloguing in Publication

Kelsey, Annie, author
Pippa Morgan's diary / Annie Kelsey.
ISBN 978-1-4431-4275-5 (pbk.)
I. Title.

PZ7.K355Pi 2015   j823'.92   C2014-904606-5

First published by Scholastic Children's Books in 2014.
This edition published by Scholastic Canada Ltd. in 2015.

6 5 4 3 2 1   Printed in Canada 139   15 16 17 18 19

Scholastic Canada Ltd.

Pippa Morgan's Diary

ALL ABOUT ME

Name: Pippa Jane Saturday Rachel Morgan (My parents only gave me the middle name Jane, but I added the other two because I think it's really unfair that we don't get to choose our own names. I mean, we're the ones who have to have them for our ENTIRE LIVES! I chose Saturday because it's my favourite day of the week and Rachel because that's the name of my BFF.)

Age: 10 (which is really cool because ten is my favourite number in the whole world — apart from infinity — but I don't think I'll ever get to age infinity!)

Height: Half a forehead taller than the hallway shelf. (I know this because I accidentally walked into the hallway shelf last week and it made a bruise right in the middle of my forehead. I didn't mind though because the bruise looked a bit like the Batman symbol.)

Favourite Colour: Indigo (I'm not exactly sure what colour indigo is — it just sounds really cool. Try saying it out loud and see: IN-DI-GO!)

Favourite Animal: I love all animals, so it's really hard to choose just one. If I had to pick, it would be a bunny-dog (that's actually my two favourite animals in one). ☺

Favourite Pop Star: Tiffany J!!!

Favourite Song: YOLO by Tiffany J.

Favourite Food: Chicken nuggets and Dad's home-made pizza.

When I grow up I want to be: An acrobatic dancer. Or a spy. Or maybe I could be an acrobatic dancer who spies? I could spy on all the people in the audience at my shows.

swallows back tears Yesterday, at 11:32 a.m.,
my best friend of all time, Rachel Adams,
moved to the other end of the world.

Have you ever lost your best friend? Well,
don't. It's the WORST.

Mum gave me this diary.

She said writing stuff down would "help me
process my feelings of loss."
???
Writing stuff down is basically *homework*,
but here goes . . .

Sunday

I can still smell the stink of the moving van. Me and Rachel just hugged and cried as they loaded her stuff on. Then I watched like a big-eyed kid who'd just lost her puppy while Rachel waved out of the window of her parents' car.

I will <u>NEVER</u> forgive Rachel's parents — I STILL CAN'T BELIEVE THEY DECIDED THAT RACHEL SHOULD LIVE IN <u>SCOTLAND</u> INSTEAD OF THREE DOORS AWAY FROM ME!

1

Scotland is, like, a gazillion miles away.

Rachel said Nothing Would Change Really. *rolls eyes* She said *We'll still be best friends even though I'm so far away*. I love Rachel but sometimes she can be one fry short of a Happy Meal.

    Of course we'll be <u>best friends</u>. But it's not the same. I can only talk to her on the landline. I don't get to *see* her every day.

We can NEVER AGAIN dress up in my dad's extra-high-visibility cycling gear and go and stand under the fluorescent lights in the supermarket and see how many shoppers we can dazzle. The frozen food section was best because the freezers had this cold *blue* glow that turned us practically luminous. We'd offer to help shoppers reach for fish fingers or ice cream and try not to giggle when they'd half-close their eyes like they were staring into the sun.

We *loved* dressing up. Last summer, we pretended we were characters from *The Lady of Morpeth Abbey* — which was our favourite TV programme EVER. It was *soooo* romantic and all the characters wore beautiful old-fashioned clothes. Me and Rachel raided every charity shop in town until we'd made the BEST costumes. Rachel dressed as Mr. Hunderbentleman (buckle-y shoes and a frilly shirt and a big hat and everything) and I wore ten *big* skirts on top of each other and put my hair in a bun so I looked like Lady Monteith, and we spent the whole day talking like our characters.

RACHEL: Lady Monteith, may I bring you something from my morning stroll as a token of my admiration?

ME: I would *be* eternally grateful if you brought me a dozen roses, Mr. Hunderbentleman, for my pretty nose needs something delicate to smell.

RACHEL: *(giggling)* My dear lady! Why don't you stroll with me and we may smell the roses together?

ME: Oh, Mr. Hunderbentleman! I am so lucky to know such a kind gentleman as you.

And we did it ALL day. Mum and Dad thought it was really funny (Mum and Dad were still married then) and it was the best day ever. Then Mum told us to go and get changed because my big skirts kept sweeping things off her knick-knack shelf and Rachel had to go home for dinner.

I wonder what Rachel's having for dinner tonight? I could have the same thing and it'd be like we were having dinner together like we used to when Rachel's mum went to yoga.

But I can't even text her to ask because she's living on the side of a mountain in the middle of NOWHERE.

Rachel's new house!

Apparently, there are more sheep than mobile phones where she lives now.

This is the first time I haven't seen Rachel for a whole day since, like, FOREVER.

But Mum always tells me to look for the good things in stuff that happens, so here goes.

7

Good Things About Rachel Moving To Scotland

1. Rachel will *be able* to make lots of new friends (*sob*).

2. Rachel might get a Scottish accent and then she can *become* an actor like she's always wanted (you have to *be* able to do accents to *be* an actor).

3. We can write each other actual real letters just like Lady Monteith and her sister, Georgina, which will *be* really cute.

4. Without Rachel, I'll have lots of extra
    time to spend on homework so I can
    become a genius and invent a way for
    mobile phones to text _anywhere_.

I guess I can *visit* Rachel. Dad asked me
where I wanted to go on holiday next year.
Why not Scotland? There aren't many good
things about your parents getting divorced,
but one of them is that you get TWO
summer holidays.

Tiffany J's parents are divorced too. That
practically makes us soul-twins. Tiffany's
watching me now, from a poster on my
bedroom wall. It feels like she can really
see me and knows what I'm going through.

9

Tiffany J is my favourite person in the whole world (apart from Rachel). In the poster she looks like Princess Jasmine from *Aladdin* with a floaty headscarf and curly shoes. She is *soooo* pretty! Who else could look cool on a camel?

Tiffany J

She's also the greatest pop star ever.
She won the *Voice Factor* last year and since
then she's had a billion hits and travelled
round the world more times than I've been
to school. She's only three years older than
me. But she owns, like, fifteen mansions
and has a driver to take her anywhere she
wants. I bet she has her own pilot too. She
must have hundreds of best friends and if
any of them moved to the other end of the
country, she'd have a zillion new ones lining
up along her driveway.

I am SO going to be like Tiffany J.

Imagine if I'd auditioned for this year's
Voice Factor. I can picture it now. The
judges are sitting behind their big neon

desk. Steven Fowl is watching me walk onstage. He has that look like he's thinking, *Yeah, well she's only ten, how good can she be?*, and then I start singing. And my voice is FANTASTIC — even better than Tiffany J's — and when I start my dance, his face lights up like someone's plugged him into a wall socket.

Karen Eastbourne's sitting next to him and her eyes are as wide as an owl's. Then the audience starts cheering me. And standing on their feet. No — they're standing on their chairs they're so excited. No one can believe I'm *that* good! All the judges are AMAZED. Cheyenne stands ON THE DESK and starts clapping.
Huey Brown is pinned back in his chair like

he's been hit by a wave.

I wish I could make this happen for real!
My life would be perfect!

Monday

I'm writing this entry in secret. I have to keep my diary under my desk, on my lap, so Mr. Bacon can't see. I've decided this diary might be a good idea after all. I don't know if it's helping me to "process my feelings" but, now I don't have Rachel to talk to, my diary is like my new best friend.

Mr. Bacon is teaching us geography. (YAWN.)

He's telling us how mountains are made. *Why?* No one's *ever* going to make one. Where would they put it?

It's horrible being at school without
Rachel. Darren's sitting
next to me instead. There's
playground grit under the
desk from his football feet

and he smells like cornflakes.
I'm trying to ignore him, but he
keeps sniffing.

Mr. Bacon is drawing a volcano on the
whiteboard, firing burning rocks into the
air. I hope that the mountain near Rachel's
house isn't a volcano. I'd better write to
her and warn her to check there's nothing
coming out of the top.

I wonder if Mr. Bacon is married. He

doesn't wear a wedding ring. I guess it's hard finding someone who wants to become *Mrs.* Bacon. It's not exactly a normal name. Unless she has a worse name, like Miss Sandwich. ☺ That would be brilliant! Their kids would be Bacon-Sandwiches!

<u>List of Funny Names</u>

Chris P Bacon

Russell Sprout

Justin Time

Stan Still

Hazel Nut

Rob Banks

Jed I Knight

Neil—

17

Break time

I'm back. I couldn't finish my list. Mr.
Bacon stopped drawing volcanoes and
started talking about eco-energy. He
decided that I should show the class
how a wind turbine works. I had to stand
up. Everyone started laughing while I
helicoptered my arms. It *was* quite funny
until I accidentally smacked Darren in the
face. He was OK
and his nose didn't
actually
bleed. But,
even though
I said sorry, he
asked Mr. Bacon

if he could sit somewhere else. Mr. Bacon said yes and let him move to Tom's table.

I don't know what's worse — Darren's cornflakes smell and football grit or sitting by myself.

They're all in the playground now. I'm the only kid left in the classroom. Now Rachel's gone, there's no one to play with, so I asked Mr. Bacon if I could stay inside and write in my diary. He said I could so long as I was quiet while he sorted out the book cupboard. So I'm pretending I'm a spy, like the ones I watched on *Spies Next Door* last night. Mr. Bacon is an enemy agent, searching the classroom for state secrets. I'm hunching low to my desk and breathing as quietly as I can. I've made a note of the books he's stored close to the front of the cupboard. They're called *Exploring Japan*. I'm guessing that's going to be our new topic once we've finished learning how to build mountains.

Guess what? Mr. Bacon just told me that after break he's going to ask Catie Brown to sit next to me!!!! ☺

Catie Brown is the most popular girl in our year. Everyone wants to hang out with her. She has an actual _SCHEDULE_ for who gets to sit next to her at lunch.

I hope she likes me.

Catie Brown

I've got butterflies in my stomach.

Later

I think Catie might actually like me. ☺ ☺

At first she wouldn't look at me. She just sat down and stared longingly at Julie Johnson's table. So I tried doing crazy doodles in my notebook so she'd think I was funny. I drew a talking carrot. And a cat in a space helmet. But she didn't even look at them.

When Mr. Bacon told us to colour in our pictures of Henry the Eighth, I told Catie where I lived and about my hamster who died and *all* my favourite TV shows.

But she didn't answer, only grunted and coloured her picture in. Then Freya, who was sitting at the table behind, leaned over. She whispered to Catie that she had seen the queue for the *Voice Factor* auditions in town.

I saw Catie's eyes light up and I knew straight away — she likes the *Voice Factor*!

"I auditioned for it." The words rushed out before I could stop them.

Catie looked at me like I'd appeared out of nowhere. "Really?" Her eyes were wide and she was staring at me. "You had a *real* audition?"

I nodded. My face felt bright red but I couldn't stop. I had her attention. So I told her everything, just like I'd imagined it last night. How the judges were blown away and the audience cheered.

And she believed me. Her eyes were popping out of her head, and then she said the magic words.

"You have to sit next to me at lunchtime and tell me all about it."

Lunch was SO scary. The twins, Julie and Jennifer Johnson, sat at our table. My mouth was so dry I could hardly speak. My mind was spinning as Catie sat down next to me and started unpacking her lunch. I was desperately trying to think up brilliant details to add to my audition story. But the twins

kept giggling and
started listing all
the things they loved
that began with the
letter J.

Juice.

Jenga.

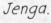

I was

trying SO

HARD to picture what Karen

Eastbourne had been wearing in

my daydream.

Jewellery.

Jeans.

Jelly.

What had Cheyenne's hair looked

like?

Jumble sales.

Jam.

Junior school.

HOW was I meant to concentrate on my story while Julie and Jennifer kept going on about J words?

<u>Things I DON'T like</u>
<u>beginning with J</u>

Julie

Jennifer

Johnsons

Then Catie asked me about the audition. "Tell me EVERYTHING."

So I started. "Karen Eastbourne was wearing jelly and Cheyenne's hair was like a jumble sale."

I KNEW I'd get mixed up!

Catie started frowning and I thought *she must know that I'm making it up*.

So I took a really deep breath and started to list as many random facts from my daydream as I could:

- The audience stood on their chairs.

- Steven Fowl was amazed.

- Cheyenne leapt off the desk and
  shook my hand when I finished.

- Afterwards, people crowded around
  me and begged for my autograph.

My brain started to ache so I took a bite
of my sandwich.

Catie offered me one of her chips. She
was all "Wow" and "That's amazing."

I got a wormy feeling in my stomach. I
hated lying to her. But it was better than
sitting by myself.

Then she said, "I wish exciting things
happened to me." And I felt like the
biggest liar in the world. If Catie knew the
truth she wouldn't want to talk to me. So

I said something that was sort of true. "I just wish Rachel had *been* with me."

And Catie said, "Rachel was your best friend, right? You must miss her."

I was relieved that I could *be* honest about *that*. I told Catie that I missed Rachel SO MUCH. And Catie told me that, when she moved up to juniors, her best friend had gone to a different school and she'd cried every day for a week.

Isn't that tragic?

We're practically twins (but *not* boring ones like Julie + Jennifer).

Mr. Bacon must have noticed because after lunch he paired me and Catie up for our class project. We've got to do a presentation on what it's like to be a

ten-year-old girl in Japan. (I am SUCH
a great spy! I *knew* we'd be doing Japan
when I saw Mr. Bacon move the *Exploring
Japan* books to the front of the cupboard
during break time.) Catie grinned at me as
he read out our names and I felt happy for
the first time in days.

Then, after school, she waited for me
while I got my lunch box and we walked out
of the school gates together. Her mum was
waving at her from a big blue car.

I stopped as Catie walked up the
pavement to meet her. I didn't know if she
wanted me following. But Catie waved me
over and asked me if I wanted to go to her
house after school on Wednesday so we
could work on our project.

Her mum was smiling at me through the open car window. She said: "It would *be* lovely if you could come, Pippa. It's always nice to meet Catie's friends."

Does this mean I'm one of Catie's friends *already*? WOOT!

Perhaps I'll end up *being* her *best* friend and I can help with her lunchtime schedule (I'll *always* sit next to her, of course!). And we can talk on the phone all the time and she'll think I'm way cooler than all her other friends. I can just imagine it now . . .

Phone rings:

MUM: (*shouting up the stairs*) It's Catie on the phone for you again!

ME: (*racing downstairs*) Thanks! (*grabbing phone*) Hi, Catie!

CATIE: I'm planning a party and everyone's coming but I want you to be the guest of honour.

ME: Wow, Catie! Thanks! I'd love to be your GoH!

CATIE: Great! I'm *so* lucky you're my *best* friend in the whole world.

☺ ☺ ☺ ☺

Laterer

Mum just told me that Dad has found an apartment! Yay! Since he moved out, he's been staying with Uncle Pete, but now he's going to have his own place! This means I can stay with him. I like living with Mum but it doesn't seem fair on Dad if I just stay with her all the time. Plus, I miss Dad's cooking. Mum tries her best but she doesn't *love* cooking like Dad does. We've been eating Fridge Surprise *a lot* since Dad left. (Fridge Surprise is whatever Mum can find in the fridge served with rice or pasta. Yesterday we had sausage curry. Today it was cheese and beetroot macaroni. I peeked in the fridge while Mum was washing up. I hope she goes shopping tomorrow *because* I'm scared what she'll make with yogurt and cauliflower.)

After dinner, Mum looked tired, so I tried to cheer her up by performing my best magic trick.

I got the TV remote so I could make it disappear then reappear behind Mum's head. But I had my floppy sweater on (the one Gran knitted for me to "grow into") so, when I snuck the remote control up my sleeve, it slid right up and flopped over the armpit-bit and, when I leaned forward to jiggle it out behind Mum's head, it skied down my back and plopped on to the floor. It was like I'd laid an egg.

Mum laughed. So did I. I like doing magic, but I'm glad I've switched to singing. I never got very good at magic. Singing is *way* more fun.

Wednesday

Ms. Allen has ordered me to wait in the changing room. My writing is wobbly because it's difficult balancing my diary on my lap while I'm holding my nose. But if I let go (of my nose), I'll choke. It smells like feet come here to die.

I forgot my PE uniform. There's no way I'm going to wear someone else's icky uniform from Lost Property so I told Ms. Allen I'd hurt my foot (which was sort of true because I stubbed my toe on the banister this morning and it REALLY hurt). But then Ms. Allen wanted to know *how* I'd hurt my foot and I didn't think she'd count a stubbed toe as a real injury (even though I bet a *real* athlete would — no one could win the Olympics with a toe as badly stubbed as mine) so I told her I'd fallen off the tightrope while I'd been practising my circus skills.

I *know*!

DUMB!

Why did the circus have to be the first thing that popped into my head? There are some BIG downsides to having my imagination.

Ms. Allen looked like she didn't believe me.

And Mandy Harrison was listening.

She said *"Circus skills?"* like it couldn't be true (I bet I could have tightrope lessons if I wanted).

Then Catie stepped forward and said: "My cousin learns circus skills after school at the community centre."

I LOVE YOU CATIE BROWN!

I nodded like crazy and Ms. Allen smiled and told me to stay in the changing room. I would have died if she'd found out I was lying. But maybe I *will* start learning circus skills one day and maybe I will hurt my foot falling off a tightrope. Then it won't be a lie any more.

Oops! Something heavy just hit the gym floor. Jane Harding probably fell off the pommel horse again.

I can't *believe* that I'm going to Catie's house after school. I'm staying for dinner too. Her mum phoned my mum. *Real* food! Mum's yogurt and cauliflower risotto wasn't the best thing I've ever eaten.

<u>Dad's Dinners I Miss Most</u>

Spaghetti Tangle

Torched Chicken

Tuna Bomb (Dad calls this his
"signature dish" and writes his name in
cheese on the top)

Mausage and Sash (that's what Dad
calls Sausage and Mash)

Pizza Faces (I always choose pepperoni
for the eyes and a big tomato mouth)

I've just got one problem. Catie wants to hear my audition song for the *Voice Factor*.

OK, I'm going to confess something, so if you've found this diary and are having a snoop, STOP READING RIGHT NOW, because this bit is REALLY PRIVATE:

I can't sing as well as Tiffany J. In fact, I can't sing at all!

I was the only person last year *not allowed* to join the Y5 choir. I told everyone that I was resting my voice for when I start proper singing lessons (which I'm definitely going to do when Mum can afford it). But really it was because Mr. Thompson said I was so out of tune that I was distracting the other singers. He put me in charge of props at our end-of-year show. It was my job to guard the technicolored dreamcoat while everyone else was rocking the hall with *Go, Go, Go Joseph!*

I refuse to speak to Mr. Thompson now. I don't think he's noticed but I always give him a hard stare when I see him. I could be *brilliant* by now if I'd done a year in the choir. Instead I just scare the neighbours. *sighs*

I don't want to scare Catie too. I'm going to have to think up an excuse when she asks me to sing.

Excuses for Not Singing

1. Tonsillitis (her mum might send me home).

2. I'm saving my voice for the next audition (*might work?*).

3. I've forgotten the words (*Catie might google the lyrics*).

4. I bit my tongue at lunchtime and it's too swollen to sing properly (*would Catie ask to look at my tongue?*).

5. I ate chilli for dinner last
   night and it burned
   my vocal cords (*she
   definitely wouldn't be
   able to see my vocal
   cords — I don't
   have a clue where
   they are*).

6. Steven Fowl made
   me sign a contract
   promising not to sing
   for anyone outside the
   Voice Factor in case I'm discovered
   by another music producer (*that
   would be so cool*).

Later

I cannot *believe* what has happened!!

By the time we got to Catie's house, I was
so nervous my heart was *beating* like a
drum machine. I felt like I was going to
the Queen's house for dinner. It didn't
help that, when we got there, Catie's house
looked like something from a *movie*. The
front lawn was practically a *carpet*. The
house was perfectly white with a shiny
blue front door. The letter box shone like
gold. There were no weeds in the garden
path like our house. And no chipped paint
around the windows.

Inside was even *more* like a movie house.

There were wide wooden floors
everywhere. They were so gleamy that I
kept expecting a Disney princess to waltz
through a doorway.

Catie's mum was really sweet and
smiley but, as I walked
in, I could see her
staring nervously at my
shoes. I thought she
must have a fear of shoes like my mum
has a fear of heights. Then I saw the
gleamy floors and guessed she had a fear
of footprints. Catie was already slipping
her shoes off so I did the same and
Catie's mum snatched them up like she
was catching mice. She hid them in the
hall cupboard with our school bags and

the hall was suddenly neat again.

Our hall is *never* neat. Catie's mum would probably faint if she saw it. There are boots and coats and bags everywhere (although there's a bit of space now, where Dad's bike used to be). Mum used to joke that our mess hid the stains on the carpet.

ANYWAY.

Catie's mum gave us juice and biscuits. I thought we'd take them up to Catie's room but we had to eat at the kitchen table. Catie whispered that it was "because of crumbs" and rolled her eyes when her mum wasn't looking.

Her mum must *be* scared of footprints *and* crumbs.

(She'd *definitely* faint in our house.)

As soon as we'd finished, Catie took me up to her room. It was HUGE. The size of a netball court with pink and white rugs. And the rugs were so fluffy! I had to take my socks off to feel them properly.

I hopped from one rug to the next. It was like jumping across marshmallow stepping stones.

Then I saw Catie staring at me with big panicky eyes. She looked a bit like her mum.

I froze. Was it against the law to take your socks off in her house?

ME: Sorry. I just wanted to feel the rugs.

49

CATIE: Really?

ME: They're so soft.

I started to reach for my socks but Catie suddenly grinned and took off her own socks.

CATIE: You're right! They're as soft as kittens.

ME: They're as soft as a rabbit's tummy.

CATIE: They're as soft as the inside of a puppy's ear.

ME: They're as soft as strawberry mousse.

We danced from rug to rug until we were out of breath, and then we collapsed on Catie's bed.

And then she said the thing I was dreading. "Do your audition piece, Pippa. Pleaaasssee!" She looked at me like a desperate puppy. I felt hot. I got up and walked to the window and looked out. There was no way I could lie to Catie while I was looking in those eyes. I was just about to explain about Steven Fowl making me sign a contract promising not to sing to ANYONE, when I saw a burglar.

A REAL-LIFE BURGLAR.

In next-door's garden, a big man was heaving a sack down the garden path. He kept glancing back at the house like he was scared he was being watched.

I ducked and flapped at Catie. "Look!"

She came over and looked out.

CATIE: That's just Mr. Briggs. He lives next door.

I peeked out of the window. There was a tall wooden fence between Catie's garden and next door's. Beyond it, I could see Mr. Briggs heave the lid off a turtle-shaped sandpit. He started scraping at the sand to make a hole in the middle.

ME: Why is he burying a sack in his garden?

Then I remembered an episode of *Spies Next Door* where one of the secret agents buried a load of top-secret files in an allotment. What if Mr. Briggs was collecting secrets for foreign governments and hiding them in his garden?

I had to find out!

I rushed out of Catie's room and ran downstairs. Catie was right behind me. As we crossed the hall, she steered me past the kitchen and through the utility room. We charged out of the back door in our bare feet and raced up the lawn.

Catie giggled. "The grass tickles!"

I don't think she'd been on the lawn in her bare feet before.

I told her to shhhhh! Mr. Briggs mustn't hear us through the fence.

I could hear him scraping away at the sand.

But how could we see over the fence?

I spotted an apple tree and pointed into the branches. "Let's climb it."

Catie glanced back at the house. "Climb a tree?" Then she looked at her school skirt. "I'll get dirty. Mum'll be cross."

"No you won't!" I pulled her towards the tree. We scrambled on to the first low branch, then the next and the next, until we were peering over Mr. Briggs' fence.

Just in time!

The sack was in the turtle and he was covering it with sand.

My brain was whirring. *What should I do?*

I was so busy
thinking, my hand
slipped and I tumbled
round the branch and
slid out of the tree. I
landed with a thump in Mr. Briggs'
flower bed. Catie gasped and stared
down at me with big owl-eyes. Mr.
Briggs spun round. He stared at me
as I sat among the flowers. Then he
looked up at owl-eyed Catie and burst out
laughing.

That surprised me.

The secret agents on *Spies Next
Door* never laugh.

I decided that he must be
pretending and jumped

56

to my feet. "What are you burying?" I said, trying to sound calm and strong.

Mr. Briggs didn't answer. He just waved Catie down from the tree. "Get down from there before your mother spots you," he told her. He caught her as she jumped and swung her down on to the lawn. "Now what are you doing?" His eyes were smiley.

I gave him a fierce look. "What are *you* doing?" I glared meaningfully at the half-buried sack.

He laughed again.

"Are you working for a foreign government?" I demanded.

Catie stared at me in horror.

But Mr. Briggs just laughed again. "I'm hiding birthday presents!" He dragged the

57

sack out of the sand. "For Harry."

Was that a code name for his boss?

ME: Who's Harry?

CATIE: His son.

MR. BRIGGS: Harry always finds his birthday presents when I hide them in the house, so I thought I'd hide them out here. Harry hasn't played in his sandpit since he was six.

ME: Why should I believe you?

Mr. Briggs reached into the bag.

ME: Watch out!

I leapt and grabbed Catie with a squeal.
I'd seen something exactly like this on
Spies Next Door. He was going to pull out
a gun and shoot us! I just knew it!

But he didn't. He pulled out a
soccer ball. And then a brand-new
Lego Mindstorms box.
He really was hiding presents!
I started blushing. I stared at my dirty feet.
"I'll get a ladder." Mr. Briggs chuckled.
"You'll need some help getting back over
that fence." He put the gifts back in the
sack and headed for the big shed across
the lawn.

Catie looked down at her clothes and I felt a prickly worried feeling in my stomach. Her shirt was smeared with green moss and twigs were sticking out of her hair. If her mum didn't like footprints or crumbs, she'd probably *hate* moss-smears and twigs. What if Catie got into trouble because of me?

As we climbed to the top of the fence on Mr. Briggs' ladder, I felt sick. Catie wouldn't want to be my friend now.

Mr. Briggs called goodbye as we used the apple tree to scramble back down into Catie's garden.

"I'm really sorry," I told Catie. Her mum was staring crossly out of the kitchen window.

I thought I was going to die when Mrs. Brown came out of the back door looking like a thundercloud in an apron.

MRS. BROWN: (*frowning*) Catie Brown! What have you been doing? (*staring hard at the moss stains on Catie's shirt*) That shirt was clean this morning!

CATIE: (*staring at her shoes*) Sorry, Mum. We were just playing.

ME: (*stepping forward*) I'm sorry, Mrs. Brown. It was my idea to climb the apple tree.

MRS. BROWN: (*eyebrows shooting up*) Climb the *apple tree*?

ME: I thought Mr. Briggs was a spy.

Mrs. Brown opened her mouth but nothing came out.

ME: It's OK. He's not a spy. He was just hiding presents and I promise I'll never make Catie get her uniform dirty again. I'm very good at learning from my mistakes.

(This is actually true. Last year I persuaded Rachel to go to the park, and when we got home, Rachel's mum was all pale and shaky and thought we'd been kidnapped and was about to call the police. We'd been playing Poo Bag and lost track of the time. Poo Bag is a brilliant game where you have to say Poo Bag! every time you see a dog walker carrying a bag with poo in. Then you score a point. Rachel and me used to play it all the time. When she moved away the score was:

Me: 38   Rachel: 32

I wonder what her score is now? Mine's 45.

ANYWAY.

Rachel's mum nearly died of fright so, after that, every time me and Rachel went out, I always went and told Rachel's mum first.)

Mrs. Brown was still staring with her mouth open so I said, very solemnly, "*I absolutely promise that it will never happen again.*"

This seemed to make Mrs. Brown's eyebrows go back into their proper place. She said, "Well, I suppose it'll all come out in the wash" and went back into the kitchen.

I looked at Catie.

She had her lips pressed together. I thought she was really angry with me, but as soon as her mum had gone, she *smiled*. "That was fun!" *That's actually what she said.* "That's the *best* fun I've had in AGES!"

Then she hugged me!

I can't believe it!

I've made a new friend. ☺ ☺ ☺

Thursday

☹ ☹ ☹

Terrible news!

(I'm squashed in a cubicle in the girls' toilets. It's not easy writing in here. I keep banging my elbow on the toilet paper holder.)

The school head, Mr. Badger, just announced in assembly that there's going to be a charity talent show at school NEXT WEEK and anyone can enter.

Normally a show would be fun. And I'd get to watch Matilda Sweet from Y6S try to sing harmony with her best friend Jasmine. I've heard cats in the garden with better voices. (They sang "I Wish

It Could Be Christmas Every Day" at
the Christmas show. By the time they'd
finished, everyone was glad it was only
once a year.) Some of the Y6 boys always
try to be the next big boy band. And the
Y4s are so cute when they sing. (In their
school assembly last term, they dressed
up as fruit to teach us about vitamins
and one of the strawberries tripped over
and couldn't get up again, so
the bananas tried to help him
and one of them fell over too
and knocked the rhubarb into the
scenery. And everyone kept singing
the Vitamin Song even though it looked
like someone had spilled fruit cocktail
on the stage.)

But nothing is *normal* now. I'm in the middle of the *biggest* lie I ever told. If my fairy godmother appeared right now and granted me a gazillion wishes, a talent show is the *last* thing I'd wish for. Why can't I have a fairy godmother? I could wish for a voice like Tiffany J's and all my problems would be solved.

Of course, Catie was bouncing up and down as we filed out of the hall. She says I HAVE to do my *Voice Factor* audition song. She says I'll totally win.

I just grinned at her lamely and wished I'd never started this dumb lie. Why can't we raise money with a sponsored walk like other schools?

I can't tell Catie I made up the whole story about my audition. She'll hate me. And she only just started liking me. She's the closest thing I've got to a bf right now. If Catie stops being my friend, I'll go back to being the loneliest girl in school.

But I *can't* sing in front of everyone. They'll think I've swallowed a cat.

My face is turning red just thinking about it.

Got to go. Louise Hawkins is banging on the cubicle.

Before dinner

I'm at Dad's new apartment. It's brilliant!
There are TWO bathrooms, a balcony outside
the living-room and a nice garden underneath.
I'm only staying for dinner tonight because
Dad has to leave early for work. But I can
sleep over at the weekend. I can't wait! ☺

I'm so glad Dad's got his own place.
Uncle Pete's house is kind of messy
(what Mum calls "bomb-gone-off messy")
so Dad used to take me out when I saw
him. (Now I know how Mandy Harrison
feels. She only sees her dad in Burger
King. She says her mum calls him the
"Lord of the Fries.") But now me and Dad

can hang out like we used to at home.
It's a bit bare though, and it's weird
that there's nothing in the cupboards
and drawers. At home I'm scared to open
anything because stuff falls out. Mum
keeps promising to "have a clear-out"
but she never does. Perhaps she should
move into an apartment too.

Dad's making Tuna Bomb while I get
settled into my new bedroom.
"Getting settled" means putting
Bobsy on my bed (which took
about three seconds), so I've
got time to write in my diary. I can
smell cheese cooking though so I'd better
hurry, Dad will be calling me in a minute

Bobsy

and I *absolutely*, totally need to write down everything that happened at lunchtime.

I could hardly *believe* it. The twins invited me to their sleepover tomorrow night. (Hanging out with Catie means I've been hanging out with Julie and Jennifer too and they're not boring at all. They don't *only* like things beginning with J — they like *everything*: cats and rollerblading and hamsters and *Spies Next Door* and prawn cocktail flavour chips. I think they might be psychic. They keep finishing each other's sentences like they're mind readers.)

So I was really happy when they invited me too. I knew Catie was going, but I never expected them to include me. I nearly choked on my yogurt when they asked me, I was so excited. I thought when Rachel left that I'd never go to another sleepover again. When I get home, I'm phoning to tell her. I wonder if Rachel's made new friends yet. I hope so. Being lonely is no fun.

Dad just popped his head round the door to tell me he forgot to buy ketchup. He's turned the oven down and gone to buy some. He'll be back in ten minutes, which means I have the whole place to myself. I'm going to do my favourite thing — put on my headphones and listen to the latest

Tiffany J album. I'll see if I can work out some dance moves to "YOLO," which is totally the BEST track.

It's hard to write with your head under a pillow but I don't care; I'm staying here forever.

I am SO EMBARRASSED.

I had my headphones on and I was working on the best dance move ever (jumping off my bed into a free spin, heel turn, kick). I was out of breath after twenty of those so I stopped to just sway to the last verse. I didn't even

realize I was singing. I certainly didn't
know I was singing so LOUDLY.

Then I heard a noise through my
headphones. Someone was behind me! I
shrieked and nearly jumped out of my
socks. I thought it was a burglar but when
I turned round, Dad
was standing in the
doorway, looking
pale, with a strange
man peering over his
shoulder. They were
staring at me like I
was on fire.

I hauled off my
headphones.

ME: What's wrong?

DAD: We thought you were dying.

STRANGE MAN: I was about to call the police when your dad came home.

DAD: Mr. Eckington lives next door. (*Dad points to strange man*) He heard you through the wall.

MR. ECKINGTON: I thought you were being mauled by cats.

ME: I was just singing.

DAD: (*looking at Mr. E*) I'm so sorry we

disturbed you. Pippa doesn't usually do this kind of thing.

MR. E: Well, that's a relief.

ME: (*blushing so hard I can't speak*)

DAD: (*smiling apologetically at Mr. E*) Maybe I can get her some singing lessons.

MR. E: (*smiling sympathetically*) That might be a good idea. She does seem very (*he pauses while he thinks of a word*) . . . enthusiastic.

ENTHUSIASTIC?
When Steven Fowl tells a *Voice Factor*

contestant that they're "enthusiastic" it's code for *terrible*.

I'm staying under this pillow all night. I'm never showing my face again.

 MAULED BY CATS!!

What am I going to do? Catie's going to hear me sing one day, even if it's only at the end-of-term assembly. Then she'll know I'm rubbish and I lied about the audition. I wish I could tell her the truth, but she'll never be my friend if I do. I'll be alone forever.

I wish I was Tiffany J. I wouldn't even have to go to school. I'd be at Centre Parcs

shooting my new pop video in the water
rapids. I'd be whizzing down flumes while
cameras filmed me, mouthing the words
to my next hit as I shot out into
a big blue pool. Music
would be thumping
and everyone would
be watching
and thinking
how cool
I am. My
personal stylist would be waiting for me
at the edge and I'd swim over so she
could fix my make-up and start restyling
my hair for the next shot. There'd be a
whole rack of clothes to choose from for
the dance number on the poolside and my

choreographer would be working out a new move that everyone will want to copy as soon as they see it.

Why can't I be Tiffany J instead of Pippa Morgan? Her life is way better.

My life is THE WORST.

Friday

Now it's WORSE THAN THE WORST!

Catie put my name on the sign-up sheet
for the talent show before registration.
   Argggghghhhhh!

She was so pleased when she told me, like
she was giving me a present. And I had to
act like I was pleased so she'd think I can
sing. She mustn't find out I was lying about
the *Voice Factor* or she'll stop being my
friend. And that would be AWFUL. She's
so nice and I feel happy when I make her
laugh.
   Which reminds me, I'd better smile at

Mrs. Gould and look interested for a bit.

Mr. Bacon is away on a training day so Mrs. Gould is teaching us about the Tudors. We've got our exercise books on our desks, so it's easy to disguise my diary as my notebook. I just have to look up every now and then so that Mrs. Gould thinks I'm listening.

Mrs. Gould is *totally* into Henry VIII. I think she secretly wishes she'd been one of his wives (not one of the headless ones). From the way she's going on about Katherine the Arrogant, I'm guessing she thinks she could have done a much better job as Mrs. VIII.

I don't know why *anyone* would want to

marry Henry VIII, although it couldn't *be* worse than being entered for the school talent show when you can't sing.

What am I going to do? If I back out, Catie will know. If I don't back out, *everyone* will know.

Yesterday, Dad managed to persuade me out from under my pillow for some Tuna Bomb. He said it was OK if I couldn't sing like Tiffany J and there were lots of other things I was good at. Like *spelling*, for instance.

Oh, great.

When Steven Fowl ditches *Voice Factor* and does *Spelling Factor* instead, I'll be fine. I can imagine the audience standing on their chairs, screaming with

excitement, while I spell ALGORITHM.
Not!!

He said I could have singing lessons if
I really wanted which was sweet. But even
the _best_ lessons in the world won't teach
me to sing by next Friday.

There must be SOME way of getting out

of the talent show. I wonder if anyone at school has tonsillitis? I could stand next to them in the lunch queue and hope they cough on me.

(Henry VIII just executed Anne Boleyn. *SO* mean! At least Mum and Dad managed to split up without anyone getting their head chopped off.)

If I can't find someone to cough on me in the lunch queue, perhaps I can catch a chill by leaving my bedroom window open at night. I know it's only September and the nights are pretty warm, but Gran complains all year about the damp getting into her bones. Perhaps it'll get into mine before the talent show. I can imagine explaining to Catie. "I can't stand on stage.

I've got damp bones." Is that why Gran
needs a walking stick? Are her bones
floppy?

Darren just told Mrs. Gould that if he
was king, he'd never get married. He said,
"Why have a wife when you've got loads of
servants?" Mrs. Gould is giving him a hard
stare.

Oops, now she's staring at me.

I had to close my diary. ☹ Mrs. Gould told
me off for doodling. Doesn't she realize
that this diary might be worth a *fortune*
one day? I can picture it being auctioned in
London . . . *one million pounds, two million
pounds, three million pounds, going for
three million pounds! Sold!* I wonder how

much Tiffany J's diary is worth? I'd give anything to read stuff she wrote when she was still an ordinary schoolgirl. I bet she had big dreams even then. She is *sooo* inspiring. I'm going to be inspiring too once I'm famous.

Quick, there's the bell! There's just time to write this before I join the lunch queue (fingers crossed that there's a cougher)!

Catie just told me that Julie and Jennifer have something REALLY special planned for their sleepover. I can't wait! Squeeeee!

Friday — midnight

I'm at the twins' house, but I can't sleep.

How can I? It has to be the most EMBARRASSING sleepover ever!

I'm curled up at the bottom of my sleeping bag, using my phone as a light while I write. I'm also eating a cereal bar. There are crumbs everywhere. (It's a good job Mrs. Brown's not in here with me.)

The twins are asleep. I can hear their parents snoring down the hall. Catie's sleeping bag is on the floor next to mine. She keeps giggling in her sleep. She's probably remembering Mr. Johnson's face when they finally managed to—

Wait! Let me start at the beginning.

Julie and Jennifer's mum walked us home from school. She's really nice. She has one of those smiley faces like TV mums, except she's not as skinny as a TV mum and she wears less make-up. She'd brought apples for us to eat on the way home in case we were hungry. (Which I was. It was "sweet and sour chicken" day at school today. I think the chicken must have dissolved because I couldn't find any on my plate and the sauce was so red and slimy it looked like it had been scraped off the scenery of *Emergency Room*. The school chef must have learnt to cook at the same place as Mum.)

Julie and Jennifer's house is more like

mine than Catie's and I was relieved that we had to climb over shoes and bags to get to the stairs.

The twins share a room. Why was I surprised that they have twin beds? It must be fun to share a room with your sister — like having a sleepover every night. The weird thing was, Julie's half of the room was really neat and Jennifer's half looked like she'd been burgled. There were clothes all over her bed and books and games sticking out from underneath it where she must have pushed them to make room on the floor for our sleeping bags. We sat in Julie's half and the twins told us about the special surprise they'd planned.

JULIE: Guess what we're going to do after dinner?

ME: Tidy Jennifer's half of the room?

JENNIFER: Ha ha. (*not laughing*)

JULIE: Shhh! I'm trying to tell you about the surprise.

Then Julie crossed the room and pulled a scarf off a lump on her desk. Underneath, there's a big, pink CD player.

Catie squealed with delight.

Jenny started beaming as happily as Julie.

I just stared at the CD player, trying to

force myself to smile. Lying next to it
was a big, pink microphone.

Karaoke!

Nooooooooooooooo!

Catie leapt to her feet
and started begging
to have a go, but Julie
said her brother was
still asleep because he's
working night shifts this week. But he gets
up after dinner and we could try it out then.

I was still staring at the machine. A
feeling of horror was creeping over me
like ice fingers. What was I going to do?
As soon as Catie heard my Voice of Doom,
she'd *know*.

I MUST NOT SING.

My mind started whirling back to my excuse list. Would Catie and the twins believe that Steven Fowl made me sign a contract promising not to sing for anyone outside *Voice Factor* in case I'm discovered by another music producer?

No! There weren't any music producers *here.*

Unless the twins' brother was one.

A spark of hope flashed through me.

ME: (*crossing my fingers*) Where does your brother work, by the way?

JULIE: (*staring at me like I've just asked*

94

if she's got a pet elephant) Why do you want to know?

CATIE: (*squeezing my arm*) Aren't you excited about the karaoke? I can hear you sing at last! It's going to be SO cool. I just hope you don't think I'm rubbish.

ME: (*my stomach has tied itself into a knot even a Girl Guide couldn't undo*) I won't think you're rubbish. (*But you'll think cats are mauling me.*)

I looked at Julie again. "Is your brother a music producer, by any chance?"

"A music producer?" Julie's eyebrows shot up. "He works at the hospital."

"Oh." I stared at the karaoke machine. "I was just wondering."

I tried eating dinner really slowly. Anything to delay the karaoke. Mrs. J kept glancing at me with a worried look and asking me if I felt OK while I pushed my peas round my plate.

Catie squeezed my arm and whispered, "Don't you like fish fingers?"

"I'm just not hungry," I replied. I wished the fish fingers were hot enough to burn my throat, but we'd taken so long getting downstairs that they were hardly even warm.

When Mrs. J started clearing the plates away, she slipped a cereal bar into my hand. "In case you get hungry later," she whispered. Catie, Julie and Jennifer were already racing upstairs, squealing with excitement. I followed them, my heart hammering like someone was doing roadworks in my chest.

"You go first, Pippa!" Catie was holding out the microphone as I entered the room. Suddenly I knew how Anne Boleyn felt on the way to the chopping block. I imagined the executioner holding out the axe and saying, "Do you want to cut your own head off?"

"No. *You* go first," I told her, trying to sound generous.

She shrugged. "OK."

Catie has a sweet voice. She was

watching me nervously while she sang, like she was singing in front of the Queen. When I clapped at the end and told her she had a really nice voice, she blushed. The twins begged her to sing another song and I was SO relieved when she did. Then they sang a duet. They can do really nice harmonies. It's like *everyone* can sing except me. I must have *been* cursed by a wicked fairy godmother when I was born. It's the only possible explanation. All the time the twins were singing I knew my turn was coming closer. As they started swaying for their Big Finish, I whispered to Catie, "I have to go to the bathroom" and rushed out of the room.

Once I was locked in the bathroom, I started sweating. How could I go out there and sing? I wondered whether to pretend I was ill and ask Mrs. J to phone my mum. But then I'd have to pretend to be sick all weekend. And I'd miss the sleepover. And they might not invite me again.

I don't know how long I'd been hiding

when Catie came and knocked on the door.
She said, "Are you OK?"

I said the first thing that came into my
head. "I'm stuck!"

"Stuck?" Catie sounded worried.

"I can't open the lock." I looked at the
old bolt on the back of the door. It looked
like the sort of bolt that would get stuck,
although I can't remember if it felt stiff
when I locked it.

"I'll tell the twins!" Catie's footsteps
hurried away.

I felt relieved for about five seconds.
I couldn't stay in the bathroom all night,
could I? I peered into the bath and
wondered if it would be a comfortable place
to sleep. I put the plug in, just in case, to

stop any spiders crawling up.

Then there were lots of footsteps in the hallway.

A deep voice called through the door. "I'm Jeff," it said. "The twins' dad. Have you tried wiggling the bolt?"

I reached out and pretended to wiggle it. "Yes, but it's too stiff."

"Don't worry, Pippa." Mrs. J was calling through the door now. "We'll get you out."

"I don't mind sleeping in here," I offered, half meaning it.

"Don't be silly." Mrs. J told me confidently. "You won't have to sleep there. Jeff's going to climb through the window and undo the bolt for you. OK?"

I stared at the window. "But it's too high

up!" How would Mr. J reach the first floor?

"He's getting the ladder out of the garage," Mrs. J called through the door.

Catie's voice sounded beside her. "Don't panic, Pippa. You'll be out in a minute."

I could hear clanking outside the window.

This was worse! If Mr. J climbed through, he'd see the bolt wasn't stuck and know I was lying, and then I'd have to sing, and then Catie would know I was lying.

I AM NEVER LYING AGAIN.

By now, I felt sick and hot. I sat on the edge of the bath while I listened to the ladder creaking outside. Then I saw a shape looking outside the glass and someone knocked on the window.

"Open up, Pippa."

I undid the latch and slowly pushed it open.

Mr. J caught hold of the frame and swung it wide. He beamed at me from outside. "Oh dear, what can the matter be?" he sang. "One young lady locked in the lavatory." I didn't laugh. I was too busy wondering why even Mr. J could sing better than me.

"It's all right, Pippa. I'll just climb in." Mr. J was already heaving himself through the window.

Mr. J is not a small man. You know I said Mrs. J wasn't skinny? Well, Mr. J is even *less* skinny. By the time he was halfway through, the window frame was pressing into his *belly* and he was starting to sweat. His face had turned the colour of our living-room curtains (Mum calls them "mauve" but they're purple).

"Um, Pippa." Mr. J sounded breathless. He'd stopped moving. "I think I'm stuck."

I stared at him. Then I stared at the door, which was supposed to be locked. I was totally trapped.

"Mrs. Johnson?" I called through the door.

"Is Jeff in yet?" she asked.

"He's stuck."

"Stuck?" (Why did people keep repeating that word?)

Mr. J hollered behind me. "I'm wedged in!"

"I told you not to have a second helping at dinner," Mrs. J called back.

"You offered," Mr. J puffed.

"I was just being polite." Mrs. J was starting to sound frazzled.

I backed against the wall, feeling that I was about to be caught in a family argument. But Mr. J changed the subject. "You'd better call the fire department."

Most people might think it's exciting to hear a fire engine come howling down the road and screech to a stop outside. And I suppose it *was* interesting to see a great big fireman appear behind Mr. J and

start easing him out of the window like
someone uncorking a bottle of wine.

But I was mostly thinking about the lock
and what everyone would say when they
found out that I'd been lying. I made a list
in my head about who would be angriest.

People Angry With Pippa

Mr. J — *because he had to be rescued by a fireman like a cat up a tree.*

Mrs. J — *because she'd wasted half her evening rescuing me, then her husband, for no reason.*

Catie — *because she realized I was a liar.*

The twins — *because I had ruined their special karaoke sleepover.*

My mum — *do I need to explain?*

So you can imagine my surprise and relief when the fireman (after he'd eased Mr. J back down to the ground) climbed back in and reached for the bolt and then <u>STRUGGLED TO OPEN IT</u>.

"It *is* stiff, isn't it?" he'd said as he let me out. Then he nodded kindly to Mrs. J and ruffled my hair. "All safe and sound. But I'd put some oil on that bolt. Or get a new one."

Mrs. J hugged me. "Are you OK, Pippa?"

I was blushing while Catie and the twins hopped around me.

CATIE: Were you scared?

JULIE: You were SO brave!

JENNIFER: Can I use the bathroom now?

Mrs. J went downstairs with the fireman and, while Jenny disappeared into the bathroom, Catie and Julie dragged me into the front bedroom so we could watch the fire engine drive away. The neighbours were outside, standing under the street lights, hugging their dressing gowns around them while they watched the fire engine drive away. Mr. J was chatting to the man next door while Mrs. J was waving to the fireman. I suddenly realized how late it must be.

"What time is it?" I asked.

Jenny appeared in the doorway.

"Ten o'clock."

"No!" Julie sounded upset. "We can't do any more karaoke. Mum said we have to stop at nine-thirty so we don't disturb next door."

I looked out of the window at the neighbours drifting slowly back to their houses, stopping for a final moment of gossip before they disappeared indoors. "I think we might have done that already."

Then I heard Mrs. J's feet on the stairs. "Come on, girls. It's been an exciting night. But it's time for bed."

I looked at Catie, feeling guilty. "I'm sorry."

Catie blinked at me. "What for?"

"For spoiling the evening."

"Spoiling it?" Catie burst out laughing. "You made it the most exciting sleepover EVER!"

Julie and Jenny started laughing too.

"What did Dad look like when the fireman pulled him out of the window?" Julie squealed.

"I bet he looked like our rabbit when it got stuck in the cat flap," Jenny giggled.

I pretended to giggle too, but inside I felt terrible. What would they say if they knew I'd made the whole thing up?

Lying is SO stressful. I'm going to HAVE to tell Catie the truth about my singing.

Sunday night

I had my first whole night staying over at
Dadville last night. (*Dadville* is my name for
Dad's new apartment. Guess what Mum's
house is called?) It felt weird to *be* in my
own bedroom even though I'm *not* in my own
bedroom. It was like I'd been split into two
people in some mad-professor experiment. I
kept wondering if, while I was sitting on my
bed in Dadville, another Pippa Morgan was
sitting in my bedroom at home.

I tried to help Dadville feel more homey
by taking two Tiffany J posters — one for
my bedroom, one for the living-room (which
is actually a kitchen and living-room joined

together. Which is kind of fun). Dad said I'd better put them *both* in my bedroom because sometimes he has friends round and it's not cool to be a Tiffany J fan when you're forty years old.

Isn't that SOOOO cute? My dad worries about being cool. He has absolutely no idea that it's impossible to be cool when you're forty.

I pointed out that Tiffany J would probably help him look cooler but Dad told me to put them both in my room anyway.

So I put one over my bed and one over my new desk (Dad bought it specially so I could do my homework when I start staying over longer).

DAD MADE PIZZA FACES!!! ☺ ☺ ☺ I had
SEVEN toppings:

Pepperoni (eyes and nose)

Tomato (smile)

Cheese (hair)

Cheese (_beard_)

Extra Cheese (moustache)

Ham (cheeks)

Sweetcorn (freckles)

Dad even remembered the garlic bread. And we watched a movie. And at bedtime he said I could keep my light on and read as long as I wanted because it wasn't a school night. Mum always makes me turn off the light at nine even on Saturdays!

Having two homes is *definitely* going to be fun.

There was one bad moment.

I was cleaning my teeth in the bathroom and I felt something tickling my leg. I thought it was just a stray hair or some fluff off my dressing gown, but when I looked down I saw that it was a SPIDER.

ON MY LEG!

A *HUGE* SPIDER.

Of course I screamed and Dad came running and started screaming too. (He's not a big fan of spiders either.) He started flapping at it with a towel while it clung to my leg like it wanted to hug me to death. Eventually, he flicked it off and it scuttled behind the toilet.

Dad *promised* he'd find it and throw it out *before* my next visit but how can I *be* sure? I can imagine it crouching behind the bathroom, rubbing its front legs together while it plans its next Pippa-attack.

It's really hard to decide where I like being the most. I like being at Dad's, but then I feel bad that Mum is by herself. But

Mum's feels like *proper* home, and that makes me feel sad for Dad because his apartment doesn't. It's SOOOO confusing! When your parents split up, your feelings split up too — I have two feelings about everything! Brain-burn!

Dadville vs. Mumville

	Mumville	Dadville
Lights on after nine p.m.	☹☹	☺☺
Pizza Faces	☹	☺☺☺
Spider attacks	☺☺☺☺	☹☹☹☹☹
Feels like home	☺☺☺☺	☹
Eating in front of the TV	☹☹	☺☺☺
My own bathroom	☹	☺☺
Mum is there	☺☺☺	☹☹☹☹
Dad is there	☹☹☹☹	☺☺☺
Total	☹ = 10 ☺ = 12	☹ = 11 ☺ = 13

118

ANYWAY.

When Dad dropped me off this morning,
Mum had great news. Catie had phoned
and wanted to come over so I could help
with her dance routine for the talent
show.

   Catie wanted to come to my house!

When she got here, I don't think she
even noticed that our front garden didn't
have carpet-lawns and our floors weren't
princess-gleamy. I showed her my
Tiffany J DVDs and we picked all Tiffany's
best moves and worked out a great dance
for Catie. She is going to totally rock at
the talent show.

After that, I had a brilliant idea. Catie had seen my Tiffany J poster (the camel one) and she really loved it so I offered to give her a Tiffany makeover. We borrowed Mum's make-up and her hair curlers and I found some floaty scarves at the bottom of her scarf drawer.

I'm not exactly good at putting on

make-up. I've tried a few times but eyeliner and mascara are very smeary and lipstick seems to want to go everywhere. Blusher is confusing too. Are you meant to put it on your cheekbones or under them? I decided to try both.

The trouble was, Catie kept flinching and giggling when I came at her with the eye pencil. And I don't think laughing when someone is trying to put lipstick on you is a good idea.

I wonder if Tiffany J's make-up artist has to sit on Tiffany while she's applying lip liner?

Anyway, I finished at last and managed to get a few curls into Catie's hair without burning her (though her hair did smell a bit cooked when I'd finished).

I was just pinning on the floaty scarves when Catie's mum arrived to collect her. Catie was really excited about showing her mum her new look. She said, "I keep trying to persuade Mum to let me wear make-up. When she sees how beautiful I look, she'll *have* to let me wear it!" And she went running downstairs.

Maybe I should have let her look in a mirror first.

Catie didn't *exactly* look like Tiffany J.

By the time I got downstairs, Mum and Mrs. Brown were staring at Catie as though she had been replaced by a bug-eyed alien.

122

MRS. BROWN: (*turning pale*) What have you done to yourself?

CATIE: (*smiling happily*) Pippa's given me a makeover.

ME: (*apologetically*) We were just trying out a new look.

MY MUM: (*butting in quickly before Mrs. Brown could speak*) For *Halloween*. That's right, isn't it, Pippa? (*staring at me with agree-with-me-now-or-else eyes*) They were trying to see how scary they could make themselves look for when they go trick-or-treating.

MRS. BROWN: (*looking relieved*) Oh. Well, that's certainly scary, Catie.

CATIE: (*looking puzzled*) Is it?

MY MUM: Why don't you wash it off before you go home, Catie? You don't want to spoil the surprise for the neighbours before Halloween.

CATIE: (*heading upstairs, still looking puzzled*) I guess not.

I went upstairs with her and when she looked in the bathroom mirror I thought she was going to have a heart attack. Mum was right. She looked more like a zombie than Tiffany J. But Catie just burst out laughing when she saw herself. She said, "No wonder my mum looked so shocked. It looks like you paintballed me!"

This made me laugh so much I got hiccups and by the time we got downstairs Mum and Mrs. Brown were chatting over a cup of tea. Catie's mum looked really pleased to see Catie back to normal and, after they'd gone, Mum was really nice about her broken lipstick and the

125

eyeshadow I'd got mixed up in her blusher. She said, "It's about time I got some new make-up. I've had this stuff for years. Why don't you keep it to practise with?"

My mum is the best!

Monday

Today started off great. If only it had stayed that way.

Catie was practising her dance routine in the playground at lunchtime. She's a really good dancer. I joined in because I know all the moves. Then we showed it to Mrs. Khan, the lunch lady, and she looked impressed. Then Catie told her that I was going to sing in the talent show and I'd made it through the *Voice Factor* audition. While I was trying not to blush to death, Mrs. Khan asked me to sing for her. Mandy Harrison heard and came to see and before I knew it, Mandy Harrison, David Furnivall, Darren, Julie, Jennifer and

Jane Harding were crowding round, all begging me to sing.

Then Mandy said, "If you're such a good singer, why haven't we heard you before?"

I used the excuse I'd used last year about the school choir — that my singing coach didn't want me picking up bad singing habits from a school choir. But all the time, my mind was whirling as I tried to think up an excuse for not singing *now*. Everyone was chanting, "Sing! Sing! Sing!"

It was like a nightmare. So I grabbed my throat and said it was sore.

Catie looked worried. "I hope it's OK for the show." And Mrs. Khan came and felt my forehead. "You do look a little pale." Then she took me inside so I could sit in the office.

I'm still sitting here, waiting for the bell to go for afternoon lessons. Mrs. Dumpleton, the school secretary, let me go and fetch my diary so I could write in it while I was waiting.

WHY DON'T I JUST TELL CATIE I CAN'T SING?

☹

Because I like having a best friend.

sighs

Tuesday

My lie to Catie has definitely exploded
out of control. *Everyone* thinks I'm going
to be in the *Voice Factor*. And the dress
rehearsal for the talent show starts in ten
minutes.

I'm hiding in the toilets. They are actually
a pretty cool place to write in my diary.
Especially now I've found a way to write
so my elbow doesn't hit the toilet paper
holder. This is the only place I can get
any privacy. I think everyone should have
their own personal pod at school — a cosy
cocoon with a comfy chair you can snuggle
into, with a soundproof door and a lock, so

that you can hide
when you need
to escape from
everyone asking you
stuff like: *What song*

are you singing at the talent
show? Is Steven Fowl coming to watch?
Why didn't you tell us you made it through
the Voice Factor *audition? When will you be*
on TV?

Oh no! Catie's outside, knocking on the
cubicle doors. Ms. Allen wants the first five
acts at the edge of the stage, ready to go
on.

What am I going to do?

I know! I'll tell Ms. Allen I can only mime today because I'm saving my voice for the actual show.

Brilliant! ☺ ☺

Later

☹ ☹ Stupid!

Why did I think Ms. Allen would let me
mime? She said, "I'm sorry, Pippa, but we
need to get an idea of the quality of your
performance."

Catie, Mandy Harrison, David Furnivall
and the twins were backstage watching
from the wings. Mr. Badger, Mrs. Gould
and Mr. Thompson were sitting out front
with clipboards, practising being judges.

Suddenly I felt like I was actually at
a *Voice Factor* audition, except this time
my imagination wasn't going to make
everything OK.

Three thoughts rushed through
my head:

1. Run.

2. Pretend to faint.

3. Confess.

But as I stared at Ms. Allen in total horror,
I could see Catie mouthing, "Go, Pippa!"
from behind the stage curtain. Then Ms.
Allen handed me the mic and switched on
the tape player.

Time slowed down. All I could do was stare
at the teachers/judges while the blood

drained down to my toes. I felt so numb I could hardly hear the intro pounding behind me. Catie was staring expectantly from the side of the stage. I had to do something.

So I did probably the worst thing I could have done.

I *sang*.

BIG MISTAKE.

I'm not sure which bit was the most
horrible:

1. The look on Catie's face when I
    started (she looked like a fast-
    forward YouTube video, her face
    flashing through disbelief, shock,
    horror, disappointment, then anger).

2. When Mandy Harrison and David
    Furnivall burst out laughing.

3. When the twins stared at each other
    and said at the same time: "She
    lied!"

4. When Ms. Allen told me (using the kind voice she saves for the Y3s) that it was very brave of me to try but I really wasn't good enough to be part of the show. I could be in charge of the props if I liked, though.

5. When I agreed to be in charge of the props (hideous flashback to guarding the dreamcoat).

6. When Catie walked away without speaking to me.

7. When the twins followed her.

My life is totally over.

Wednesday

Catie didn't answer her phone last night. Or reply to my texts. Mum told me to give her some time. She said that Catie was probably feeling hurt that I'd lied to her. (I told Mum everything as soon as I got home from school. She gave me the biggest hug but it didn't stop the awful feeling in my chest like my heart was breaking.) Mum said that, if Catie was the nice girl she seemed, she'd forgive me soon enough.

So when I came to school today, I was half hoping everything would be back to normal.

When I walked into the classroom before attendance, Catie was sitting at a different table from the one she shared with me. She'd swapped with Darren so she was back at the twins' table with Freya. I'd be spending the day with Darren's cornflakes breath and football grit again. ☹ I tried to catch Catie's eye, then the twins', and then Freya's, but they just carried on talking to each other like I didn't exist. They all looked so happy and they kept laughing but no one talked to me.

Except Mandy Harrison. She said,
"Here's the world's greatest singer! Pippa
Morgan, our *Voice Factor* contestant. Come
on, Pippa! What did Steven Fowl *really* say
when he heard you sing?"

David Furnivall joined in. "He probably
couldn't speak because he was too busy
laughing."

Then Mandy and David collapsed
in giggles.

I hoped Catie or the twins might stick
up for me. But they just stayed huddled
round their table with Freya like nothing
had happened.

I thought I would dissolve into the floor
like a wet bath bomb, but then Mr. Bacon
came in and started taking attendance and

then lessons began and I didn't get the chance.

At break time, I couldn't face the playground so I asked Mr. Bacon if I could stay in the classroom again and write in my diary. Mr. Bacon looked at me sadly and asked if I was still missing Rachel. My eyes got hot and prickly when I said yes. Then he said, "I thought you were starting to make friends with Catie and the twins?"

That's when I asked if I could go to the bathroom because I didn't want him to see me cry. I'm still here waiting for my eyes

141

to stop looking so red. I'd better go and splash some cold water on my face before the bell rings.

Lunchtime

I'm glad I've got my diary to write in while
I eat. I don't care if my ketchup drips on
it. I'm sitting by myself, of course. I guess
I'm off Catie's schedule forever. Her table
is full. Catie is way more like Tiffany J than
I am, with a gazillion friends lined up to
take my place.

I wish she'd let me explain.

I've tried to imagine this horrible feeling
away all morning. After break I pretended
I was Tiffany J and that I was just visiting
the school. I gave everyone big, happy
smiles, and if anyone whispered when I
passed them, I told myself that they were
just whispering about how great I am.

But it's hard to keep imagining I'm Tiffany J while Catie's sitting three tables away, giggling with Julie, Mandy and Freya. I bet Tiffany's never been ignored in her whole life.

I'm going to go and stare out of the cloakroom windows. If I'm very lucky I might spot a passing circus; then I could run away with it and never come back.

Friday

Mum's right. Being sad won't make anything better. I'm not going to think about Catie today, even though she's still avoiding me. When the *bell* went for break, I came to the bathroom to write in my diary. Jenny was checking her hair in the mirror when I walked in and she actually said hi to me and asked if I was OK.

   I blurted out that I was really sorry I'd lied to Catie, and Jenny said that Catie was upset *because* she thought I was her friend and friends don't lie to each other.

ME: I didn't *mean* to lie to her. I just felt so lonely after Rachel left and Catie wouldn't speak to me until she thought I was a *Voice Factor* contestant.

JENNY: (*looking thoughtful*) Why didn't you tell her the truth before the rehearsal?

ME: Because I knew she'd be angry with me and I didn't want to lose her friendship. I really like her. And you and Julie.

Jenny just nodded, like she was busy thinking, and went back to the classroom.

At least I had a chance to tell someone how I feel. I guess I just have to get used to being alone. I'll write Rachel a long letter tonight. I know *she* still likes me. And I might as well try and enjoy the talent show. At least I'm still part of it, even if I'm just making sure everyone gets the right props before they go onstage. I might be so good at it that I end up working in showbiz. What if I was in charge of Tiffany J's props? Or even her *costumes!* I can hear her now: "Pippa, bring me my sparkly dress! And have you ironed the floaty scarves? Really, Pippa, you're fabulous! I don't know how I'd manage without you."

I'd have to go on all her world tours because she wouldn't trust anyone *else* to look after her wardrobe. Maybe one day I'll even *design* her costumes! Wow! I'd never thought of that before. I bet I'd make a great costume designer! ☺☺☺

There's the bell. Gotta go.

Later

That was the BEST SHOW EVER. ☺☺☺

   I was standing in the wings with a clipboard, next to a pile of pom-poms and Darren's ventriloquist's dummy. I'd already given the Y4s their cardboard lollies. (They sang the Oompa Loompa song from Willy Wonka. They were all painted orange. SO CUTE!)

I'd held up a mirror so the Y6 boys could check their hair before they performed "I Love You Whatever" and I had just given

the Y6 cheerleaders their pom-poms when
Catie tapped me on the shoulder.

CATIE: Jenny told me what you said. (*She
was chewing her thumbnail so I knew she
was nervous.*) And you're right. I did only
talk to you because I thought you were
going to be in the *Voice Factor*. I'm really
sorry about that.

ME: (*panicking because it sounded like
she'd only ever liked me because of the
Voice Factor thing*) It's OK. I mean, you
don't have to be sorry. I'm the one that lied
and you've been so kind to me and I only
wanted to be your friend. After Rachel went
away I thought I'd never have a friend again

and then I met you and (*I choked up now. It was like everything was washing over me like a bucket of cold water.*) I've been wanting to tell you the truth for ages but I was scared that you'd stop being my friend. I'm *really* sorry I messed everything up.

I ran out of breath. And words. So I shut up and waited for Catie to go back to her real friends.

But she didn't. She stared at me for a bit. Then her eyes started to well up. "Oh, Pippa!" And she hugged me.

Then she gave me a tissue so I could wipe my nose and she hugged me again. Then she said it was OK.

Not just "OK" OK — like people say
when they want to avoid an argument — but
REALLY OK.

ME: Do you still want to be my friend?
(*my heart was beating louder than the*
music thumping from the school hall)

CATIE: Of course! (*hugging me again*) You're so much fun to be around.

ME: Even though I lied?

CATIE: You have a big imagination. And you were lonely and feeling bad. And I kind of *made* you lie by ignoring you, which was really mean of me. But I didn't know you then. I'm really lucky that you wanted to be my friend so much because I'm so BORING! But with you, my life is much more fun! I climbed a tree because of you and we're about to go onstage and perform in front of the whole school.

ME: (*my heart dropping into my shoes*) We?

CATIE: You can dance with me! You taught me all the moves.

(By now the Y6 cheerleaders had stopped thumping around the stage and were filing past us into the wings.)

ME: (*heart zipping back into my chest and feeling lighter than it's done in days*) You really want me to dance with you?

CATIE: (*laughing*) As long as you promise not to sing.

Then she grabbed my hand and swung me onstage.

Ms. Allen stared at us from the far

side of the stage like we'd gone mad and hijacked the show. But it was too late. Our music was already playing.

The dance was a bit of a blur but it must have gone well because the crowd cheered at the end. The twins were whooping and the audience were clapping. Then Catie was tugging my hand as she bent into a low, sweeping bow. I bowed too and Ms. Allen started flapping her hands in the wings, telling us to get offstage so that

Darren and his ventriloquist's dummy could follow us.

After the show, Jenny and Julie were bouncing around us, telling us how great we were. Then the judges announced the winners and guess what? We came second!

I *Know*, right?

SECOND!

Then the end of school bell went and Catie's mum arrived and we told her about our dance and coming second and she offered to take us out for pizza to celebrate.

After-school pizza is the best. Especially when you're sharing it with your new best friend. I was a bit nervous in

the restaurant at first *because* every time
I took a *bite* of my breadstick, I'd send
crumbs showering over the tablecloth. But
Mrs. Brown doesn't *seem* so worried about
crumbs in restaurants and she let us eat
as many breadsticks as we liked.

MRS. B: I didn't know Catie was a good
dancer. She never dances at home.

CATIE: I'm scared I might *break*
something.

MRS. B: Then why don't you practise on
the lawn. There's plenty of space there.
(*she winks*) Then you could keep an eye

on Mr. Briggs at the same time, in case
he starts burying more things in Harry's
sandpit.

I was about to blush, but Mrs. Brown
laughed so kindly it was impossible to feel
embarrassed.

Then she dropped me off at home,
where Mum was watching a wildlife
documentary. I told her all about the show
and how Catie had forgiven me and how
we did the best dance ever. Mum hugged
me and told me I was brilliant, then I
grabbed my diary and snuggled in beside
her to write while she drifted back to
baboon spiders of Borneo.

What an amazing day.

Dancing in front of an audience was
EPIC. I can't believe I ever wanted to be a
singer.

I still can't believe we came SECOND! And
it was only our first performance. Imagine
how good we'll be if we keep practising.
I don't think I'll bother being a costume
designer now. Not when I love dancing SO
MUCH.

I can imagine us at Wembley Stadium. Me
and Catie are leading an acrobatic dance
company. The crowd are watching us from
the shadows while spotlights pick me and
Catie out from the troupe. I kick up my

heels into a graceful handstand and hold
it while Catie leaps up and lands so that
she's standing on the soles of my feet. She
balances there, then gracefully lifts one leg
and pirouettes. I turn
slowly beneath her so
we're moving like a
ballerina pirouetting
on a mirror.

Mum's just asked
what I'm writing
about. I told her
about the acrobatic
dance troupe and

she rubbed my hair and said, "Your imagination is so big I worry that you'll fall into it one day."

Perhaps I will, but I don't care. My big imagination is one of the reasons Catie likes me. I guess I'll always make stuff up but there's one thing I'll never do again:

I'll never lie to my new best friend, Catie Brown. (Except maybe next week when she comes over for a sleepover at Dadville. I was planning to tell her that he's just staying in the apartment while his mansion is being decorated. I like to imagine he's a secret millionaire. I bet Catie will too.)

Top ten reasons why
Catie and I are BFFs

1. We dance really well together — so well we even win prizes!

2. We both like Tiffany J (although Catie doesn't like her quite as much as I do. No one likes Tiffany J as much as I do!)

3. I help Catie do exciting things, like climbing trees and bungee jumping out of helicopters over shark-infested oceans (we haven't actually done that last one yet . . .)

4. We laugh LOADS when we're together — even when things go wrong. Especially when things go wrong!

5. Catie lives in a perfect movie-style house, but she doesn't mind that my house looks like a jumble sale that's been trampled on by a herd of elephants!

6. We both like walking on tickly things in our bare feet.

7. We do awesome school projects together.

8. Catie actually thinks that my disasters are funny, and she never sighs or rolls her eyes at me like certain teachers I could mention!

9. Catie says that I'm "fun to be around."

10. Catie is really forgiving and kind.

YOLO by Tiffany J

YOLO

You know

So let's go

Have fun!

You only live life one time

So make sure it's a fun time

Join in with this cool rhyme

And come and dance with me

YOLO

You know

So let's go

Have fun!

You only live life one time

So get out in the sunshine

Party till it's night-time

And sing this song with me

YOLO
You know
So let's go
Have fun!

You only live life one time
So make it one long playtime
Join me up on cloud nine
And have some fun with me

YOLO
You know
So let's go
Have fun!

PIPPA MORGAN'S
SLEEPOVER ESSENTIALS

- Your own pillow — other peoples' pillows always feel like they are filled with stones. Why is that?!

- A flashlight — in case there's an alien invasion in the night and they cut off all the electricity. Or you need to find your sweets during the midnight feast.

- Sweets for the midnight feast.

- NON-CHOCOLATEY sweets for the midnight feast. Chocolate melts and gets everywhere — it doesn't matter how quickly you eat it. One time, when I brought a bag of chocolate buttons to a sleepover at

Rachel's, I woke up with chocolate stains all over my pyjamas. It looked très gross! (Très is French for VERY!)

★★ Your coolest pyjamas — even if they aren't the comfiest. My hero, Tiffany J, says she always wears her coolest pyjamas when she's away on tour. And going to a sleepover is a bit like being on tour because you're away from home and . . . and . . . yes, you're away from home.

• A Tiffany J CD — she does awesome sleepover music — especially her song *BFFs Forever*.